This Ladybird book
belongs to

. . . .

LADYBIRD
TALES
OF
SUPER
HEROES

WITH AN
INTRODUCTION BY
DAVID
SOLOMONS

CONTENTS

Introduction
by David Solomons

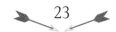

The Legend of Hua Mulan
A tale from China

Hanuman, Demon Fighter
A tale from India

Inanna in the Underworld
A tale from Ancient Sumer

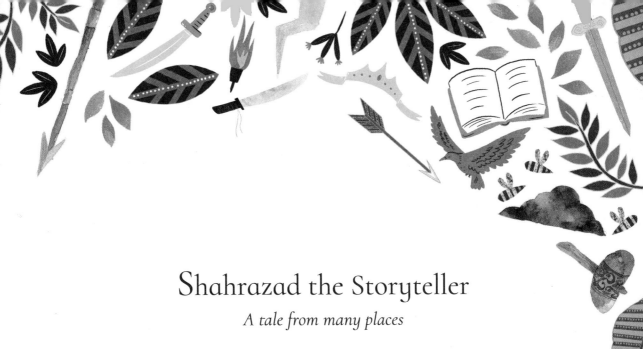

INTRODUCTION

"Great Free Gift!" yelled the headline. I was seven years old, and in my eager little hands was the latest issue of my favourite superhero comic, complete with the promised gift: a Spider-Man mask. I say "mask", but paper engineering back then was, shall we say, basic. So, for the next week, I leaped about slinging imaginary webs with a paper bag over my head.

I dreamed of having superpowers. I poked every Scottish spider I found, hoping to get nibbled by one that'd been exposed to radiation. I quizzed my mum and dad, trying to get them to reveal the truth of my origins: that I'd been sent to Scotland from Krypton as a baby, and when I came of age my powers would be activated by my bar mitzvah.

The following year, *Star Wars* exploded into the world like a poorly defended Death Star, and I found a new superhero in Luke Skywalker. I spent every waking minute straining to move my Lego with the power of the Force. It was not to be.

Every Saturday, I watched *Dr Who*, following the adventures of a Time Lord fighting for what's right across the universe – a superhero in any language (even Dalek).

As I grew older, the dream never really went away. I was always searching the skies for the ripple of a cape. Then, one day, a superhero did come into my life – one of my own creation. That superhero and his brother changed my life, so that's why I'm particularly pleased to introduce you to the characters in these tales.

If you imagined that being a superhero was all about super-strength and super-speed, then you only know half the story. You won't find the Dark Knight or the Man of Steel in this collection, but you might discover their distant relations – not capes-and-Lycra superheroes, but definitely super. Take Mulan, who trains all her life to fight but must disguise herself in order to carry out her mission (utility belt not included). Or Shahrazad, who overcomes evil using an unexpected superpower. (Hint: superpowers aren't always a result of accidental gamma-ray exposure.)

Here are six fantastical tales to thrill, amuse and make you gasp with wonder. There are magical hammers, supervillains, impossible odds and dazzling feats of bravery.

Now, you must excuse me. My super-senses are tingling, the Commissioner is on the line and I think that searchlight in the sky might be for me. Where did I leave that paper bag?

David Solomons

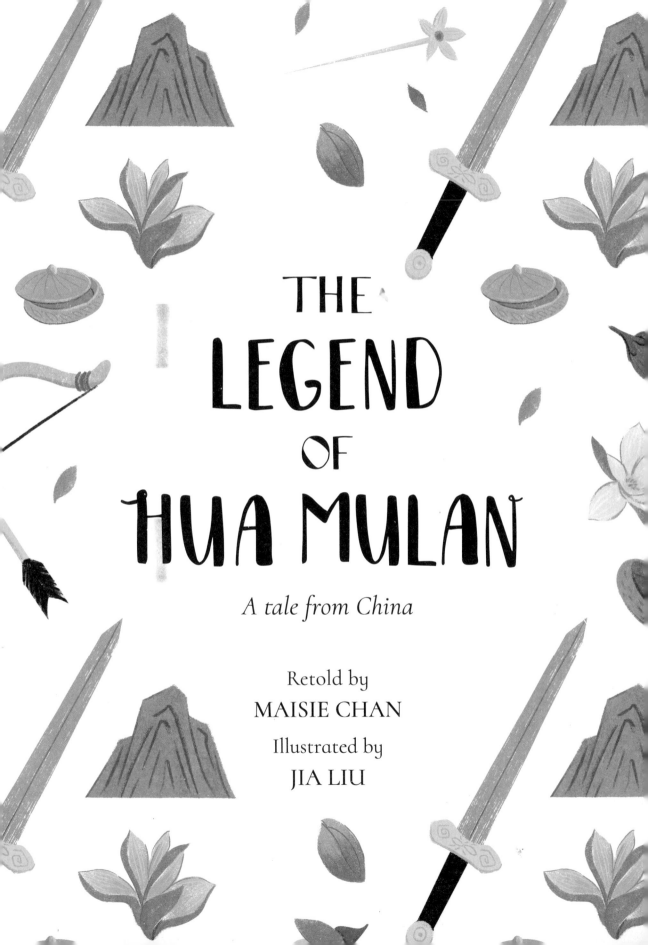

THE
LEGEND
OF
HUA MULAN

A tale from China

Retold by
MAISIE CHAN

Illustrated by
JIA LIU

n China many centuries ago a legend was born. This is her story.

Long, long ago, a soldier named Hua returned home from war, and planted a lily magnolia tree in his front garden. In the tree's tenth year, white-and-pink flowers blossomed and Hua's wife gave birth to a baby girl. They named her Mulan, after the Chinese word for this beautiful flower.

The years passed and Mulan grew into a strong and brave young woman. When she wasn't helping out by washing clothes and weaving baskets, she loved to spend time outside with her father. Mulan had a knack for taming wild horses, and she was quick to learn many styles of martial arts, including swordplay and fighting with a lance.

"You never know when you might need to defend yourself and your family," her father told her.

One day, in the marketplace, Mulan noticed a poster on a wall. It said that the Imperial Court was going to war, and each household had to send one man to fight.

When Mulan saw her father's name on the list, her heart almost broke in two. Her father had been a fine soldier in his youth, but old age and illness meant that he was no longer able to fight. She knew that if he went to war he would die on the battlefield.

Mulan, however, was fit and strong as a bison. Her body was flexible, she had excellent stamina and her senses were finely tuned. While training with her father, she had learned to fight blindfolded and with one hand behind her back. Mastering the sword had come easily to her, and shooting arrows at a target was one of her favourite pastimes.

Mulan knew there was only one thing she could do to save her father's life.

She confided her plan to her younger sister.

"I will take his place. My skills are equal to those of any man."

"But Baba will never let you go instead of him!" her sister exclaimed.

"Then it shall be our secret," said Mulan.

"Someone will notice you're a girl," said her sister. "Look at your long hair! Look at your pretty make-up!"

"Don't worry," Mulan replied. "I know just what to do."

Mulan tied her long hair up on top of her head. She carefully removed her make-up. She set her own clothes to one side, then put on her father's old armour, piece by piece.

Her sister watched in wonder as Mulan transformed into a soldier before her eyes.

Mulan felt different, too, standing there in her father's armour. Its metal protection made her feel courageous, as though she could defeat any army.

"You look like a man!" her sister said.

"I do," said Mulan. "But that's not really what matters. What matters is what's within." She patted her chest. "In here is the heart of a warrior. Clothes do not tell you who the person is inside."

Crying, Mulan's little sister hugged her goodbye. "I will tell Mother and Father what you have done. I will tell them that you'll come home safely. They will be so proud."

Mulan took the sword that had belonged to her father and to his father and to his father before him. She galloped away on a strong horse that she had tamed that summer.

She rode with a group of men from the nearby towns who were also on their way to join the army. They crossed the fast-flowing Yellow River, riding hard towards their destiny.

When they reached the spot where the army waited, Mulan signed her father's name on the contract.

"You will sleep over there," said the soldier who took her contract, hardly glancing at her. She was just another young man in an army of thousands.

She smiled as she lay down in her bed that night. Her disguise was working.

The next day, the army rode off to fight the invaders. Each day, Mulan fought bravely. Each night, she ate and shared sleeping quarters with her comrades, telling stories of her homeland but never once revealing her true identity. With each battle she fought, her courage grew – and so too did her reputation. She soon rose through the ranks to become a general, and led thousands of men in many battles.

During one of the fiercest battles, Mulan spotted one of her soldiers in the distance. He was trapped in a valley, surrounded by the enemy. Mulan dug in her spurs and charged on her horse towards him. With her sword raised high, she fought off a dozen men. She lifted the man on to her horse, and together they rode to safety.

Time after time, the soldiers hailed the mighty general as the hero they had all been waiting for. Tales of Mulan's bravery and courage spread through the ranks, but not one single person guessed her secret.

For twelve long years, Mulan served in the army in her father's place.

Mulan's younger sister worried that her sister had been killed – or, worse, that her true identity had been discovered. She was terribly afraid that Mulan would be punished if anyone found out, but no one ever suspected a thing.

After the war ended and the invaders were driven away, Mulan was brought before the Emperor.

"I have the honour of offering you the position of Commander of the Imperial Army," the Emperor told Mulan.

Bowing, she replied, "Thank you, Your Highness. However, my only wish is for a swift horse to take me back to my village."

"Are you sure?" the Emperor asked. "Is there nothing you desire?"

"Only to see my family again," Mulan replied.

The Emperor granted Mulan's wish, and she rode back to her childhood home. When she spotted her family in the distance, she saw that her parents had grey hair and her little sister was now a woman.

"I am home," Mulan declared. She took off the armour that had protected her in battle, and hidden her true identity, and changed into her old robes. Her father cried with joy as she returned the ancestral sword to its rightful spot over the fireplace, and thanked her for fighting in his stead.

Mulan's parents and her sister were delighted to see the medals she had won, and they longed to hear the stories of her battles. To celebrate her eldest daughter's return, Mulan's mother served a magnificent feast for the entire village.

Some months later, a group of men from Mulan's regiment came to visit their old general.

Their faces filled with surprise as Mulan greeted them in her pretty dress and make-up. "My name is Mulan, but you knew me as your general," she said. "I led you in battle, but now I've come home and I don't need my armour any more."

The soldiers laughed at themselves. How had they never realized their general's secret? Then they bowed in respect to the woman who had saved their lives and their country.

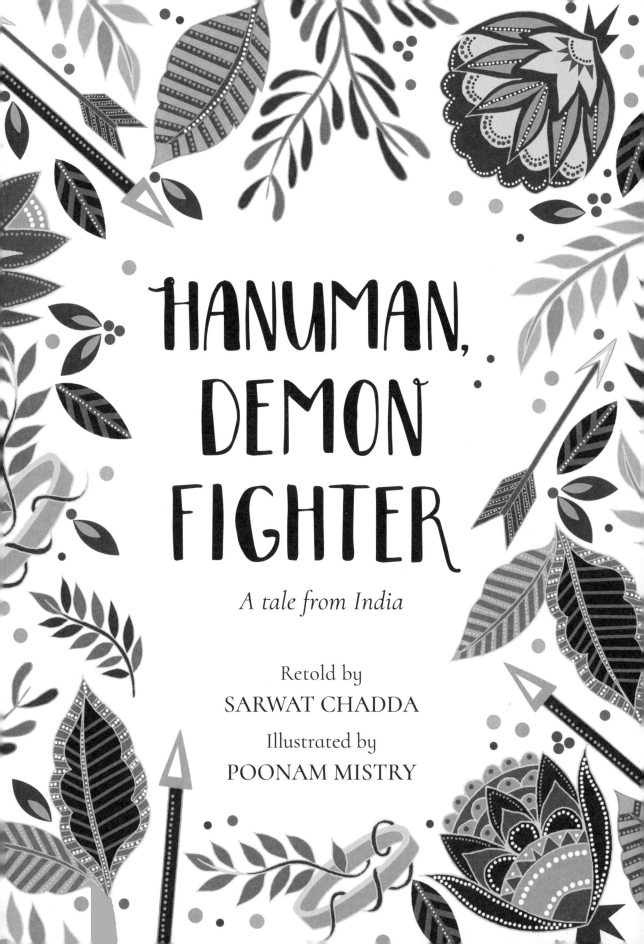

HANUMAN, DEMON FIGHTER

A tale from India

Retold by
SARWAT CHADDA

Illustrated by
POONAM MISTRY

Sugriva the Monkey King watched as two young men approached. They walked like noble princes and they were armed to the teeth, but they were dressed in rough clothes. Were they spies in disguise? What were they doing in Kishkindha, the monkey kingdom? It was very suspicious!

"Hanuman!" Sugriva summoned his second-in-command. "Disguise yourself as a man and see what they want!"

Hanuman bowed, then changed his shape so he looked like a human dressed in rags.

He approached the two men. "With your glowing skin, you look like kings," he said, "but your hair is matted and you're wandering in a forest. What brings you here?"

"I am Rama," said the elder of the two. "This is my brother, Lakshmana. We are hunting the wicked demon King Ravana, who has kidnapped my wife, Sita."

Hanuman could sense that they were good men, and he wanted to help them – especially against the terrible King Ravana, who was so monstrous that he scared even the gods. He had ten heads and twenty arms, and it was said that he could not be killed. If you cut off one head, another just popped up in its place.

"If you help King Sugriva, we will help you find your wife," said Hanuman, and before their eyes he transformed into his true shape. "I am Hanuman, and I have many powers. I am at your service."

"I will do anything to get Sita back," said Rama. "What does Sugriva want?"

"His brother has stolen the throne of Kishkindha," Hanuman explained. "Help us defeat him and restore the rightful king to the throne. Then all Sugriva's armies will be yours!"

Rama did not disappoint: he defeated Sugriva's brother with ease, and the Monkey King took his throne again.

Sugriva ordered his armies to find Sita, and millions of monkeys surged across the land like a blanket of red and gold fur. They searched every inch of almost every country, until they came to a vast ocean.

"That way lies Lanka, land of the demons!" called a vulture circling overhead. "I saw Ravana take a woman there. She was so beautiful, she looked as though she belonged in heaven!"

"That must be Sita!" said Hanuman.

The monkeys cheered. They were getting close! There was just one problem.

"Who can cross this vast ocean?" a monkey cried in despair.

"My father is the god of the wind," said Hanuman. "I can leap across it!"

He clenched his muscles and willed his body to grow. Soon he was as tall as a house, then as tall as a palace. His tail swished back and forth like a gigantic, hairy snake.

"I need to see where I'm leaping," he boomed. He climbed to the top of a mountain, then he crouched down and leaped.

As he sailed over the blue-black depths, he felt a sudden tug on his tail. What was that? He looked down. A ferocious demon with a gaping mouth had grabbed his shadow by the tail. He paused to slay the horrible creature, before sailing onwards through the air to land with an earth-shuddering thump in Lanka.

Hanuman saw the twinkling lights of a palace. He shrank himself down to the size of a tiny mouse and sneaked inside. He crept into every room in the lavish palace, until at last he found Sita.

She was alone, and her face was streaked with tears.
"Why are you here, monkey?" she asked.

"I have come to find you." Hanuman showed her a ring
that Rama had given him.

Sita cried out with joy when she saw it. "Oh, Rama!
Is he coming?"

"As soon as I tell him you are here," promised Hanuman.

He crept back outside, and swelled to an enormous size.
As he roamed the palace gardens, he uprooted trees and
smashed shrubs with his giant tail, trying to attract the
attention of Ravana. He wanted to cause the demons of
Lanka trouble and pain, and perhaps find a way to end
all this struggle.

Soon, the demons came running. Hanuman killed each
of them with a swipe of his mighty paw.

"I am Hanuman," he bellowed, his voice filling the air
so that everyone could hear for miles. "I am the son of the
wind, the killer of enemies, the servant of Rama! I'm giving
you one last chance, Ravana. Return Sita or we will
destroy your city!"

Ravana growled, "Never! Put this monkey to death!"

The demons set fire to Hanuman's tail, but he laughed and used the fire to set the buildings of Lanka alight. As he bounded away, he called, "I'll be back. And you'll be sorry!"

Again, he made his giant leap across the sea. "I have found Sita!" he told Rama. "And I know all of Lanka's weaknesses. You might find that some of the defences are ever so slightly on fire." He gave a cheeky smile. "We can attack with ease!"

"Let us cross the ocean and rescue Sita!" cried Rama.

"Let us destroy the foul demon Ravana!" cried Lakshmana.

"He truly deserves it," said Hanuman, looking down at his scorched tail.

The monkey army crumbled whole mountains into boulders and built a bridge to cross the ocean. They surged forward in their millions, with Rama and Lakshmana at their head.

The demons were ready for them. The two armies clashed in a mighty battle.

"I'm hurt, brother!" cried Lakshmana.

Rama rushed to his side. "We need healing herbs!"

Hanuman took another giant leap over the battlefield to a mountain covered in herbs. "Which one will heal Lakshmana?" he wondered aloud, then he shrugged. "I'll just take the whole mountain."

He carried the mountain to Rama on his mighty shoulders, and Rama picked the herb that would heal his brother.

The battle raged on. Hanuman threw the mountain at one of the demons. It hit home with a satisfying crunch.

Ravana and Rama were at the heart of the battle, fighting with magical weapons. They unleashed so many arrows at one another that they blotted out the sun. Finally, Rama chose an arrow from his quiver that was a gift from the gods. It flew straight and true into the demon's heart, and Sita's captor lay dead. The battle was over.

"Since you helped bring about this victory," Rama said to Hanuman, "you can give Sita the good news yourself."

The monkey smiled. "Not bad for a monkey," he said to himself, as he bounded away to find Sita. "Not bad at all."

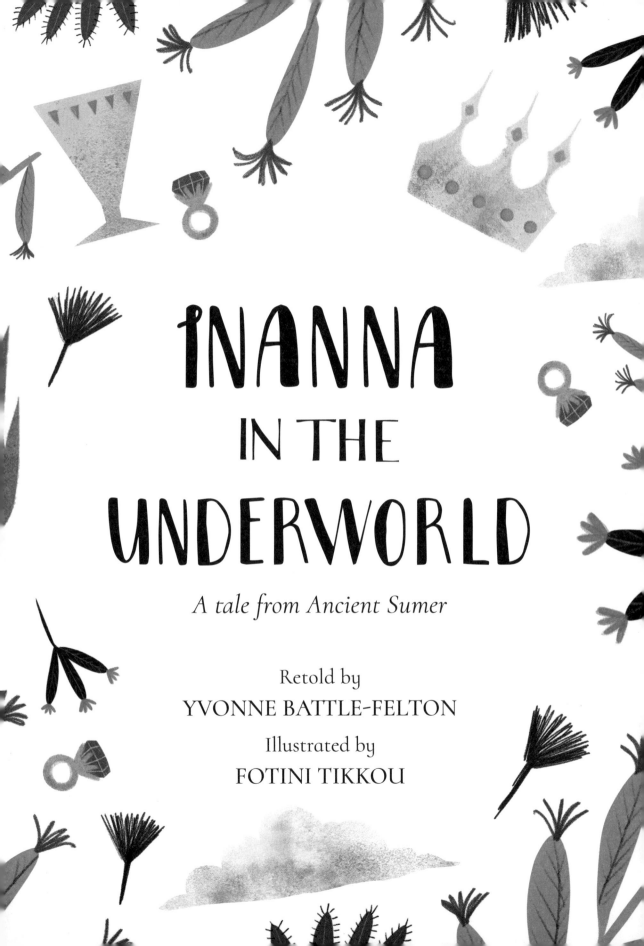

INANNA
IN THE
UNDERWORLD

A tale from Ancient Sumer

Retold by
YVONNE BATTLE-FELTON

Illustrated by
FOTINI TIKKOU

Inanna, Queen of Heaven and Earth, sat on her throne. She called for more pillows. Ninshubur, her servant and closest friend, brought more pillows. Inanna fidgeted. She leaned forward, then pushed back. She just couldn't settle.

"Something is missing," said Inanna. "I know all there is to know about heaven and earth, but there's one place I have never been."

"Do you mean the underworld?" Ninshubur asked. She hoped that she was wrong, but she already knew where this was leading.

"You do know me so well." Inanna smiled. It was a beautiful, mischievous smile that worried Ninshubur very much.

"Your sister, Ereshkigal, won't like it," Ninshubur said. "She's not the most welcoming goddess. And she's in mourning for her husband."

"Then I must go down and pay my respects."

Ninshubur saw that the idea had taken hold. "Please, Inanna, don't go," she said. "No one returns from the underworld."

As soon as she said it, Ninshubur cursed herself.

"No one returns?" Inanna liked nothing better than a challenge. "We'll see about that! I will go immediately."

Ninshubur sighed. "There will be trouble. Shall I prepare for battle?" she asked.

"No," Inanna said. "You must stay here. If I do not return in three days' time, I will need your help from above."

Inanna gave Ninshubur detailed instructions that her friend hoped she would not need.

The goddess then got dressed for her journey. She looked divine. She wore a long, lustrous wig, a royal robe, a shining breastplate, a glittering crown, a beaded necklace, a golden bracelet, and in her hand she carried a measuring rod and measuring line. Each of these things would protect her and give her strength. Inanna strode up to the gates of the underworld and banged on them, demanding to be let in.

"Who are you?" Neti, the gatekeeper, asked.

"I am Inanna, Queen of Heaven and Earth. I come to pay my respects. Let me pass," Inanna commanded.

"I must consult my queen," Neti replied.

When Neti found her, Queen Ereshkigal was furious. She knew her sister had not come to mourn. *So why is Inanna here?* she wondered. *Perhaps all of heaven and earth are not enough. Perhaps she means to rule the underworld as well.*

"Well, let us see what she has to say for herself," Ereshkigal muttered.

Ereshkigal told Neti, "Bolt each of the seven gates of the underworld, and only let my sister pass through each gate when she removes one of her protections."

Ereshkigal meant to humble and weaken her sister.

At the first gate, Neti said to Inanna, "Take off your crown."

"Why?" asked Inanna.

"To gain, one must lose," he warned. "Do not question the ways of the underworld."

At each gate, Inanna was forced to give over another one of her protections, until finally she was powerless. But she was not humble.

She entered the throne room, and strolled straight over to her sister's throne. Before she could sit down, however, she was surrounded by the Annunaki, the judges of the underworld.

"Guilty!" they howled. "We find you guilty! You are here to take over! Invader! You do not belong!"

Before Inanna could resist, they froze her to the spot.

"You will stay here in the underworld forever," said Ereshkigal. "Since you like it so much."

When Inanna did not return after three days, Ninshubur grew worried.

She followed Inanna's instructions carefully. First, she begged the god Enlil for help. Enlil would not help her. She then begged the god Nanna for help. Nanna would not help her.

Finally, in desperation, Ninshubur turned to the god Enki.

And, to Ninshubur's surprise, Enki agreed to help, even though Inanna had only recently stolen stone tablets containing the knowledge of the gods from him.

Gods aren't always logical, Ninshubur thought, *but sometimes they can be kind.*

Out of dust, Enki created two beings that were neither male nor female. He gave one of the beings food that would give life, and the other water that would give life. To both, he gave instructions.

The beings then transformed into flies, and flew through all seven gates of the underworld. Once inside, they took their true shapes, and went to Ereshkigal. She had fallen sick and was in great pain.

Whenever Ereshkigal's body hurt, the two beings cried out with her. Whenever her mind hurt, they cried out with her. Whenever her heart hurt, they cried out with her.

Ereshkigal was touched by their kindness and sympathy. She offered them a gift.

"Ask for anything," she told them. "It shall be yours."

"We want Inanna," they replied in unison.

Ereshkigal scowled, but she'd made a promise, so they were taken to Inanna. They dripped the water of life between her lips, and fed her the food of life, so that she was no longer frozen.

"Ninshubur sent us," they told her. "We're here to take you home."

Inanna cried out with joy.

"Not so fast," said the Annunaki. "You cannot leave the underworld unless you send someone to take your place."

Inanna thought for a moment. "Everyone above thinks I am dead," she said. Then she turned to Ereshkigal. "Send your guards to take the first person they find who isn't mourning me."

So the guards went up to the surface. Everywhere on earth, people mourned Inanna. Even the animals were in mourning. The guards went higher. Everywhere in heaven, people mourned Inanna.

Everywhere, that is, except Inanna's palace. There, her husband, Dumuzi, wore magnificent clothing and was throwing a party. He was even dancing.

"That's it!" Inanna howled. "He's going down to the underworld!"

But, as she rose back up to the surface, Inanna came upon her husband's sister.

"Please, let me go in his place!" the woman cried.

Inanna sighed. "I suppose a little mercy never did anyone any harm," she said.

She agreed to a compromise: Dumuzi only had to spend half the year in the underworld, while his sister took the other months.

Inanna returned to heaven, feeling a little sad about her husband. She'd miss him, in spite of everything.

But, when all was said and done, her trip down into her sister's realm had been a great success. Now, as well as being the Queen of Heaven and Earth, she also knew the secrets of the underworld, having returned from the dead.

"I told you I could do it," she said to Ninshubur, who was once again at her side.

Ninshubur smiled. "I never doubted you for a moment," she said. "But maybe . . . don't do it again?"

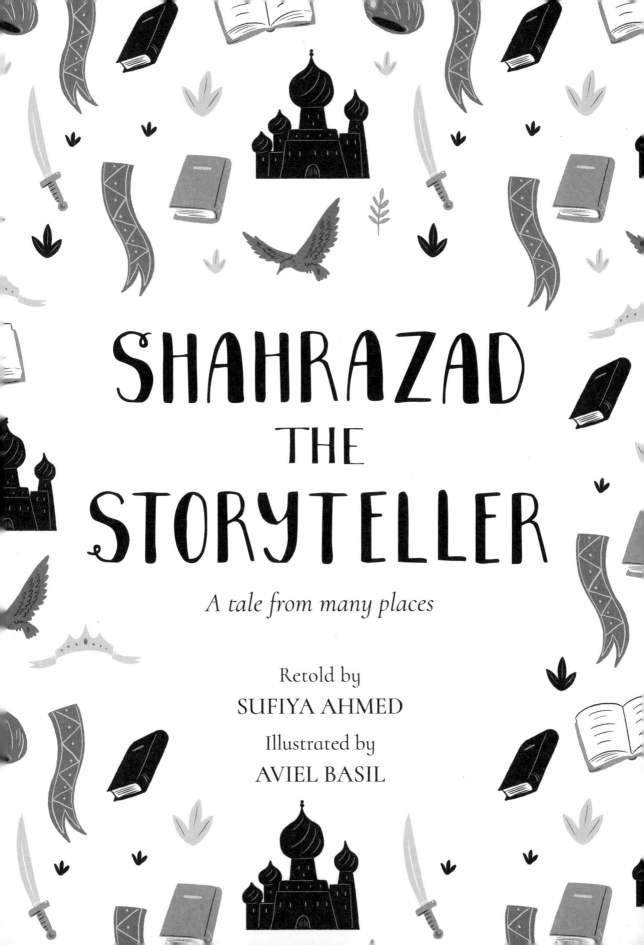

SHAHRAZAD
THE
STORYTELLER

A tale from many places

Retold by
SUFIYA AHMED

Illustrated by
AVIEL BASIL

Shahrazad was a very clever young woman who lived with her younger sister, Dunyazad, and their father, a royal minister known as a vizier.

Late one night, Shahrazad found her father sitting by the fire looking extremely sad.

"What's wrong, Papa?" she asked.

"Oh, my beloved daughter." He gazed at her, tears shining in his eyes. "It is time I told you the truth about your future. Many years ago our King Shahriyar had a beautiful wife whom he loved very much. One day he returned home early from a hunting expedition to find his queen with another man.

"King Shahriyar felt betrayed. In his fury, he ordered that the Queen's head be chopped off. Then, vowing he would never trust a woman again, he decided to marry a new queen each day and behead her the following morning. The King has been doing this for so long now that our land is running out of women for him to marry. He has ordered all the ministers to present their own daughters as brides."

"Don't cry," Shahrazad said, throwing her arms around her father.

"How can I not?" her father said, with a sniff. "I am dreading the day he will ask for your hand in marriage. After he has killed you, he will ask for your sister's hand, and then I will be left a father to dead daughters."

He started to weep again, and there was nothing Shahrazad could do to console him.

Much later, after her father had fallen asleep, Shahrazad paced the room. She did not fear her own death, but her heart sank at the thought of Dunyazad's. Shahrazad's mind whirred with ideas to save her sister and the rest of the women in the land.

As the birds began to sing with the rising sun, Shahrazad went outside to stare at the morning sky. She had come up with a plan. It would require her to be brave. It would require her to be clever. But she was ready.

At breakfast, Shahrazad told her father, "It is time for me to marry the King."

"No, it is too soon!" her father cried. "It might be your fate to become a dead queen, but, please, let us delay the inevitable!"

"Nothing is inevitable, Papa," Ṣhahrazad replied. "I have a plan to change the fate of all the women in this land. Just promise me one thing. At midnight on my wedding day, be sure to send Dunyazad to me."

Her father promised, although he did not see what good it would do.

The next day, Shahrazad married the King.

As they stood on the steps of the palace, waving to the crowds, the King was surprised at the lack of fear in his new queen's open, honest gaze. She intrigued him.

It is a shame, he thought, *that I will only know her for one night. In another world, we might even have been good friends.*

That night, after the wedding celebration, the King led Shahrazad to his bedchamber. Seconds later, there was a loud knock on the door.

"Who dares to disturb us?" the King shouted.

Dunyazad appeared in the doorway. "Forgive me, Your Highness," she said. "I wish simply to bid my sister farewell."

Shahrazad ran to embrace Dunyazad before the King could object. "Dear sister, before we say goodbye let me finish the tale of Aladdin and his wonderful lamp." She turned to the King. "May I?"

"Very well," the King said grudgingly.

Soon, he found himself completely engrossed in the story. The way his new wife wove her words into worlds was like a magic spell. The scenes seemed to play out in the room in front of his eyes, in vivid colours.

"Do you know any more stories?" the King asked when Shahrazad finished.

She nodded, and began telling him about the adventures of Sindbad the sailor. Just as she reached the most exciting part, she yawned.

"I must rest now," she said. Then she lay down on the bed, and promptly went to sleep.

The next morning, the royal executioner knocked on the door to do his duty.

"Not today!" the King shouted. "I have to find out what happens to Sindbad. You can chop off her head tomorrow."

All day, the King could think of little else but the story of Sindbad.

That night, after Shahrazad finished the tale, the King smiled. "That was very good. I could learn about courage and daring from the sailor."

"You are already full of courage and daring," Shahrazad said, flattering him. "You should hear about the adventures of Ali Baba and the forty bandits."

"Tell me," the King commanded.

Shahrazad yawned. "Not tonight. I must sleep."

The King sent the executioner away. The following morning, the King sent the executioner away again. He wanted to hear the tale of Ali Baba. He sent the executioner away the next morning, too, and the next, until eventually 1,000 nights had passed.

On night number 1,001, the King asked Shahrazad for another tale.

Shahrazad's shoulders drooped. "I have no more left, my king. I have told you all the tales from my papa's library. Tales about courage and daring, about love and compassion, and, above all, about mercy and hope. Alas, I have none left."

"Your tales have given me much pleasure," the King said. "I will grant you one wish. Whatever you want, it will be yours."

"Chop my head off if you must," Shahrazad said, "but spare the lives of the other women in this land. They do not deserve to die."

"You do not deserve to die, either," the King said. "You are the bravest and cleverest woman I have ever met. From this day, you will stand by my side as Queen. A king cannot rule on his own. He needs a friend to advise him on how to be a just ruler."

King Shahriyar and Queen Shahrazad lived happily together.

To celebrate the birth of their first child, the King built a new library for all the people in his land.

Stories were for everyone.

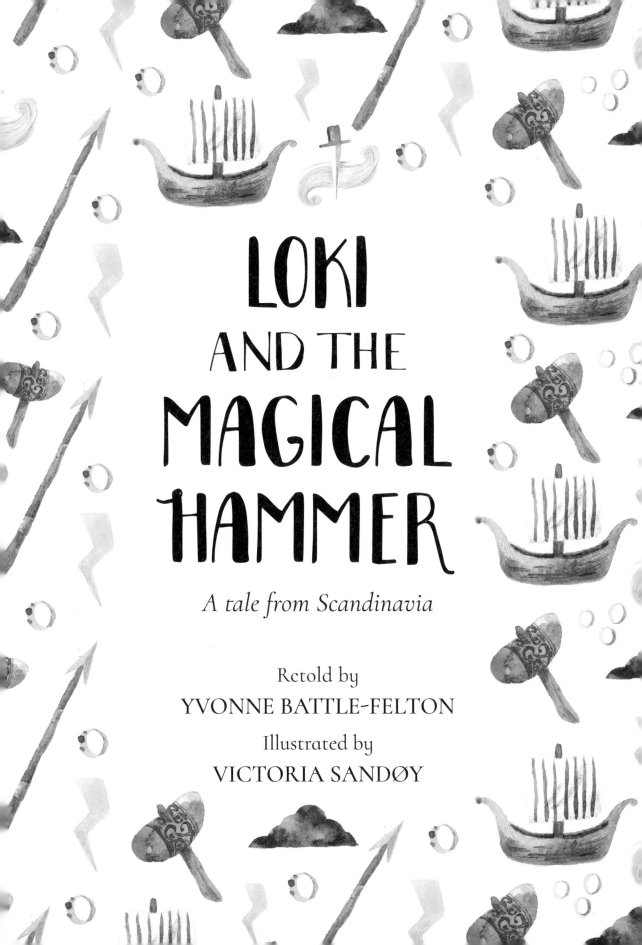

LOKI
AND THE
MAGICAL
HAMMER

A tale from Scandinavia

Retold by
YVONNE BATTLE-FELTON

Illustrated by
VICTORIA SANDØY

Thor, the god of thunder, loved adventure. His idea of a perfect day was a battle against ice giants in the morning, followed by a pleasant afternoon spent with his wife, Sif, in the beautiful realm of Asgard, home of the gods. Every day, Thor told his wife that she was even more beautiful than she had been the day before. Each morning, before he left to go adventuring, he would make a list of all the things he adored about her. The list usually began with her golden locks of hair.

Loki, the trickster of Asgard, saw Thor's boundless adoration of his wife, and had an idea. It was a terrible, spectacular idea. Loki would play a trick on Sif and Thor.

Loki rarely cared about what might happen after his tricks. It was the tricks themselves that made him grin wickedly, and he was so excited about this latest idea that his wide smile nearly split his face in two. He knew this trick would be legendary.

Knowing better than to play a trick on Thor when he was within striking range, Loki decided to wait for the mighty god to head off on his next adventure. Loki was so impatient, he could barely stand it, but wait he did. It felt like an age.

The next day, Thor set out to defend the realms. Before leaving, he ran his hands through Sif's hair.

"Your hair is as gold as a . . . crown made of gold," he said. Thor was a mighty fighter, but he was not a very imaginative poet.

Then off he went to fight some giants.

Sif spent the morning washing and oiling each strand of her hair, so that it would be especially lustrous when Thor returned. By afternoon, she was sleepy, and drifted into a deep slumber in a sunny meadow.

Loki got to work.

He had been watching from behind a nearby tree, and now sneaked up on the sleeping Sif. He snipped off each and every one of her glorious locks. He bundled the hair up and crept away.

Sif never even stirred.

Thor returned victorious. He was eager to see his wife, but she was not at home waiting for him. She was hiding.

When Thor found Sif, she was distraught. All of her hair was gone! Thor listed all of the things he loved about her, including her bare head, but it was to no avail. Nothing he said would bring the light back into her eyes.

Without her hair, Sif had lost her joy. She refused to let the other gods and goddesses see her, and declared that she would leave Asgard.

Furious, Thor vowed to find whoever had stolen her hair and make them suffer.

He didn't have to look far.

Locks of hair littered the path to Loki's door. Thor tore that door off its hinges.

"Loki!" he roared. "You stole Sif's hair!" He lifted the trickster into the air with one muscular arm. "Now you must pay!"

Loki knew that he had gone too far. "I can fix this," he said.

"How?" Thor growled.

"I will get the dwarves to weave Sif a beautiful new head of hair," Loki promised. "It will be even more beautiful than her old hair."

Thor considered this, but he didn't lower Loki to the ground just yet.

The dwarves were renowned throughout the realms for their craftsmanship. Thor knew that if anyone could make hair that would bring the smile back to Sif's face, it was the dwarves. He also knew that if anyone could convince the dwarves to complete this task it was Loki.

Thor put Loki down. "Bring me back the most beautiful head of hair I've ever seen, or I'll make mincemeat of you!"

"You won't regret it!" called Loki. He was already running towards the land of the dwarves.

It didn't take Loki long to charm a group of dwarves into weaving some beautiful hair for Sif. They also gave Loki a ship that always had wind in its sails and could fold into the palm of a hand, and a spear that never missed its mark.

These gifts were truly glorious. They would surely please the gods, and put Loki back in their good graces – until his next trick.

"But what if I can get even more gifts for the gods?" he thought.

Loki never did know when to stop. So he made a bet with two brothers, Brokkr and Sindri. He bet they could not create more magnificent gifts than the other dwarves had. He teased and goaded them, and offered an irresistible prize if he was wrong: his head.

The brothers were master crafters, and they were sure that they would win the bet. "He's going to regret this," they chuckled.

While they forged with gold, magic and skill, Loki changed into a fly to try to distract them. But, despite his trickery, the brothers succeeded. They created a magical ring that spat out even more golden rings each night, and a mighty hammer called Mjölnir that always aimed true and returned to the hand that threw it.

Now it was time to decide which gift was the best. Loki returned to Asgard, with the dwarves in tow.

Loki gave the hair to Sif. As it magically rooted to her scalp, the light returned to her eyes. He gave the magical ring to Odin, the king of the gods, who said it was very fine.

Next, Loki gave Mjölnir to Thor, who was delighted. He threw the hammer as hard as he could, and it came sailing back to his hand.

"Don't you think the handle is a little short?" suggested Loki.

"I don't care what it looks like," said Thor. "It'll crush giants with no trouble, and I'll always get it back."

The gods all agreed that the gifts made by Brokkr and Sindri were the finest, which left Loki in a sticky situation. He was about to be minus one head.

The brothers began to sharpen their axes, but Loki cried, "Wait! If you want my head, you'll have to cut my neck." He added slyly, "And my neck wasn't part of the bargain."

The gods all agreed that he was right. He'd only promised the dwarves his head.

Loki had lost the bet, but he lived to trick another day.

ANANSI
THE
SPIDER-MAN

A tale from Ghana

Retold by
YVONNE BATTLE-FELTON

Illustrated by
LOUISE WARWICK

ong ago, there were no stories in the world. Even Anansi, son of the sky god, had no stories to tell. His father, Nyame, kept them all locked inside a box.

Anansi looked around the world and said to his wife, Aso, "If we had stories, the world would be a brighter place. If we had stories, the children would laugh every day."

"You're not the type of man to wait for stories to fall from the sky," Aso replied. "Go and convince your father to free the stories!"

So he did. Anansi was shaped like a spider, so he spun a ladder and climbed all the way up into the sky.

"Please share the stories with the world," Anansi said to his father.

Nyame's laughter filled the skies. "You don't get something for nothing, my son. Fetch me the python Onini, who can crush a man with a squeeze of his tail, the Mmoboro hornets, whose stings are like a raging fire, and Osebo the leopard, whose teeth are like spears. Bring me these gifts and I will give you all the stories of the world."

"I will," said Anansi – but he knew he would need help.

Fortunately, Anansi was a very clever spider with a very clever wife. Anansi and Aso plotted and schemed all night long. By the time the sun rose the next day, they had cooked up a plan.

Early in the morning, Anansi set out with a long stick.

"How can she know better than me?" he said loudly. "I'm sure I'm right." He continued talking to himself as he walked, until he was beneath the python Onini's favourite tree.

"Why are you chattering so?" Onini asked.

"It is my wife," Anansi began. "You won't believe how wrong she is! She claims that you aren't the longest snake in the world. She says even my walking stick is longer. How can I prove to her that she's wrong?"

"Why don't you measure me?" Onini said, feeling quite insulted that Anansi's wife thought he was shorter than a walking stick. He slithered down from the tree and lay on the ground next to the stick. He was nearly as long as it.

"She is right," Anansi said, with a sigh.

"Harrumph! I *am* longer than the stick," replied Onini. "I just need to stretch out!"

"Why don't I tie your tail to the end of the stick to help you?" suggested Anansi.

Onini agreed, and Anansi tied his tail to the end of the stick with some web.

"You're certainly *nearly* as long as the stick," said Anansi.

Onini could not bear to be shorter than the stick. "Why don't you use your web to attach my head to the stick, too?" he said. "That will stretch me even further."

Anansi quickly spun the thread. Onini was indeed the same length as the stick. However, he was also stuck fast.

Anansi carried the python to his father, while Onini muttered and spluttered with rage.

"Well done," said Nyame. "Two more challenges to go."

Anansi did not stop to rest.

On the way to the Mmoboro hornets' nest, he filled a hollow gourd with water and made a plug for the hole. When he reached the hornets' nest, he poured the water into it.

The Mmoboro hornets were furious. Their home was ruined! They flew after Anansi, ready to sting him all over, but he cried, "The monsoons! The rains have come! Find somewhere to shelter, my friends!"

The hornets became worried. "You must help us, Anansi!" they cried.

"All I have is this gourd," Anansi said, "but you are welcome to it."

Whoosh! The hornets flew, one after the other, straight into Anansi's trap.

Once they were all inside the gourd, Anansi plugged the opening. The hornets' frantic buzzing shook the gourd from within, but they could not escape.

He took the gourd full of hornets to his father. "There you go," he said.

His father smiled. "Impressive. You've brought me two out of the three gifts I asked for. But catching Osebo the leopard won't be so simple."

"Who says I like things to be simple?" said Anansi.

He climbed down and dug a pit in a lush part of the forest where Osebo the leopard liked to hunt. The pit was deep and muddy. The clever spider covered the opening with branches, leaves and dirt. Then he rested by a nearby tree to wait.

After the sun set, Anansi heard a crash. The crash was followed by a loud roar.

"I have fallen into a trap," Osebo howled. "Help me!"

"I would gladly help you," said Anansi. "But how do I know that you won't eat me as soon as you escape?"

"You have my word. No harm will come to you if you help me," Osebo promised.

"Very well," said Anansi. He bent a long, green tree down into the pit. Then he flung a spiderweb down on to Osebo's tail. "Stick yourself to the tree," said Anansi. "And I will get you out."

Osebo did as he was told, and stuck his tail on to the tree, using Anansi's web as glue. "What now?" said Osebo.

Anansi let go of the tree, flinging the leopard up out of the pit. He soared up and up into the sky, free of the tree, and all the way to heaven. The leopard found himself in a tangled heap at the feet of Nyame. Anansi was just behind him, scrambling eagerly up to heaven on one of his silken spider-ropes.

Nyame chuckled. He reached behind him and brought out a beautiful box, covered in carvings. Inside, Anansi could hear the stories hissing like pythons, buzzing like hornets and roaring like leopards.

"Here," said Nyame to Anansi. "You deserve this."
He handed his son the box of stories.

Anansi took the box, and put the story you've just read inside it for safekeeping.

When he got back down to earth, Aso clapped her hands. "We won!" she said.

Anansi and his wife opened the box to share the stories with everyone. The children laughed at the stories. The adults wept and smiled, and the world was a brighter place forever.

ORIGINS

Every superhero has an origin story, but where did the heroes in this book come from? And what makes them super?

Hua Mulan
Special powers: disguise and fighting skills
Hua Mulan is a legendary warrior from China. Her story has been retold many times, in poems, plays and films. The story in this book is based on the poem *The Ballad of Mulan*, written around 1,500 years ago.

Hanuman
Special powers: changing size and super-strength
The story of Hanuman the monkey god retold in this book comes from the Indian epic the *Ramayana*. As well as having amazing superpowers, Hanuman is a very loyal and selfless friend to Rama, the *Ramayana*'s hero.

Inanna
Special power: cheating death
Inanna is a goddess who was worshipped in the Middle East from about 6,000 years ago. Her story in this book is taken from a 4,000-year-old poem called *A Hymn to Inanna* by the poet-priestess Enheduanna.

Shahrazad
Special power: storytelling

This cunning hero appeared in *One Thousand and One Nights*, an enormous book of folk tales from the Middle East and beyond. These stories were collected over hundreds of years, from many countries, including India, Iran, Iraq and Egypt.

Loki
Special powers: shape-shifting and playing tricks

Loki is a mysterious trickster god from Scandinavia. His stories – and the stories of his fellow gods – were first written down around 1,000 years ago. The story in this book was based on an Icelandic work called the *Prose Edda*, put together by a scholar called Snorri Sturluson.

Anansi
Special powers: spinning webs and being cunning

Anansi the spider is a hero of many folk tales told by the Akan people of Ghana. There is no single book that the Anansi stories come from. They're what are known as oral tales: stories told out loud and handed down through the generations by word of mouth.

"BEWARE; FOR

FEARLESS,

I AM  AND THEREFORE POWERFUL"

– Mary Shelley's *Frankenstein*

LADYBIRD BOOKS

UK | USA | Canada | Ireland | Australia
India | New Zealand | South Africa

Ladybird Books is part of the Penguin Random House group of companies
whose addresses can be found at global.penguinrandomhouse.com

www.penguin.co.uk   www.puffin.co.uk   www.ladybird.co.uk

Penguin
Random House
UK

First published 2019
001

Introduction by David Solomons
"The Legend of Hua Mulan" retold by Maisie Chan, illustrated by Jia Liu
"Hanuman, Demon Fighter" retold by Sarwat Chadda, illustrated by Poonam Mistry
"Inanna in the Underworld" retold by Yvonne Battle-Felton, illustrated by Fotini Tikkou
"Shahrazad the Storyteller" retold by Sufiya Ahmed, illustrated by Aviel Basil
"Loki and the Magical Hammer" retold by Yvonne Battle-Felton, illustrated by Victoria Sandøy
"Anansi the Spider-Man" retold by Yvonne Battle-Felton, illustrated by Louise Warwick
Copyright © Ladybird Books Ltd, 2019

Printed in Italy

A CIP catalogue record for this book is available from the British Library

ISBN: 978–0–241–38194–6

All correspondence to:
Ladybird Books
Penguin Random House Children's
80 Strand, London WC2R 0RL

MIX
Paper from
responsible sources
FSC® C018179